Some words about London:

"COO"
Cooey

"GULP!"
A piece of cheese sandwich

"GOBBLE!"
A piece of ham and ham

"CRUNCH!"
A Cheesy Snip

"Squawk!"
A raven

"TAXI!"
Nanny

More Daisy adventures!

Kes Gray

DAISY

and the trouble with

LONDON

RED FOX

RED FOX

UK | USA | Canada | Ireland | Australia
India | New Zealand | South Africa

Red Fox is part of the Penguin Random House group of companies
whose addresses can be found at global.penguinrandomhouse.com.

www.penguin.co.uk
www.puffin.co.uk
www.ladybird.co.uk

Penguin
Random House
UK

First published 2022

001

Edited by Natascha Biebow at Blue Elephant Storyshaping
Text design by Kim Musselle
Printed in Great Britain by Clays Ltd, Elcograf S.p.A.

A CIP catalogue record for this book is available from the British Library

ISBN: 978–1–5291–2998–4

All correspondence to
Red Fox, Penguin Random House Children's
One Embassy Gardens, New Union Square
5 Nine Elms Lane, London SW8 5DA

To Benji

CHAPTER 1

The trouble with London is it's absolutely FULL OF PEOPLE!

There's people on the pavements, there's people on bikes, there's people in cars, there's people in taxis, there's people in buses, there's people on the Tube, there's people in the shops, there's people walking fast and people walking slow, there's even people sitting on the pavement! London has got people ABSOLUTELY EVERYWHERE! Which is why my nanny and grampy got lost.

If you ask me, Nanny and Grampy shouldn't really go to places like London if they are going to get lost. Especially if they are going to get lost without me. Getting lost can be a very worrying thing to happen to someone, especially if they're really old. Double especially if the weather is really hot. WHICH ISN'T MY FAULT!

Today was the first time I've been into London EVER! And the first time I've ever been on a train! Or a Tube! I think it's probably been the best day of my life. (Apart from the bit when Nanny and Grampy went missing.) But it's OK, they are home safely now. I'm not sure they'll ever go into London again though. Or get on a train, or a Tube. Which is a bit silly really, because it was their idea to take me to London in the first place! Because it's the summer holidays. And they thought my mum needed a break.

A break from what, I'm not really sure?

CHAPTER 2

I'd been looking forward to today since last Tuesday! That was when my nanny and grampy came round for dinner.

The trouble with Nanny and Grampy coming for dinner is if you're having pizza, there might not be enough pizza toppings to go round.

Me and Mum have started making homemade pizzas on a Tuesday. Well, we don't exactly make the bottom bit of the pizza – the shop does that – but we definitely choose all the toppings that go on top. My favourite pizza toppings are cheese, ham and more ham. My mum's favourite toppings are cheese,

5

ham, pineapple, mushrooms and rocket. (Not a space type rocket, lettuce type rocket. No astronauts.)

Luckily I got to choose my toppings first.

It was when we were putting our toppings on that Nanny and Grampy asked my mum if they could take me into London for a day.

Mum said they could take me into London for a week if they wanted, which was a joke, only not a very funny one. Grampy said the Tower of London has a lovely dungeon I could stay in, which wasn't a very funny joke either. Honestly, just because I accidentally

coughed on the ham before anyone got to choose their toppings. How was I to know no one would want any ham on their pizzas after I'd coughed on it? It tasted all right to me.

Anyway, once Mum had said it would be all right for them to take me into London we all went into the lounge to eat our pizzas and work out all the arrangements.

The trouble with arrangements is they can take quite a long time to

arrange. After all, if you're going to go to London you have to decide what day is the best one to go, what train is the best one to catch, what places are the best ones to visit, what clothes are the best ones to wear, and what sandwiches are the best ones to take.

Nanny said she was getting her hair done on Wednesday but any day after that would be fine. So Mum chose Thursday.

Grampy checked the train times on his phone and said that the cheapest tickets were for trains that set off after 9.18 in the morning. (Going into London on a train can cost absolutely loads, especially if you buy too-expensive tickets.)

Nanny said that the 9.18 might be really crowded so it would be better to catch the one after that. Grampy said that there are lots of places "of historical interest" to visit in London. He said we could visit Buckingham Palace and Westminster Abbey and the Houses of Parliament and the Tower of London all in one day if we wanted to. (My nanny and grampy used to live in London, so they know where everything is and how to get there, too.)

Mum said the weather forecast was "set fair" for the rest of the week, so summer clothes should be fine. Nanny said that we should all take rain macs just in case. Then she said it would be a good idea if we all took sandwiches with us too. And a drink.

No wonder too! Do you know how much it costs to buy a sandwich in London? Eighty-three pounds and sixty pence! Do you know how much a drink costs to buy in London? One hundred and thirty-seven pounds and ninety-nine pence! And that doesn't even include the straw!

Honestly, my grampy knows things about London you just wouldn't believe!

After Nanny and Grampy had gone home, Mum told me that London is definitely a very expensive place to visit, but Grampy was exaggerating a bit about the cost of food and drinks.

Never mind, I knew exactly what sandwiches I was going to take with me. You've guessed it! Cheese, ham and ham. I couldn't decide on a drink, so my mum said she would surprise me!

CHAPTER 3

I slept in my clothes last night. (Not including my rain mac.) The last time my mum let me do that we were going on holiday the next day on an actual plane to actual Spain! This morning I was going on a train to actual, actual London!!!!!

By the time my nanny and grampy arrived in their car, I'd already been waiting by the window for about two hours. I had my school bag on my back, I had my rain mac in my bag, my sandwiches in my lunchbox and my Fruit Shoot in my hand. That's right, my mum bought me a Fruit Shoot to take into London with me! Not any old Fruit Shoot either, a blackcurrant one! Blackcurrant Fruit Shoots are one of the best drinks you can take anywhere because not only are they a change from plain ordinary orange squash, but the stopper on the top of the bottle is specially designed for travelling.

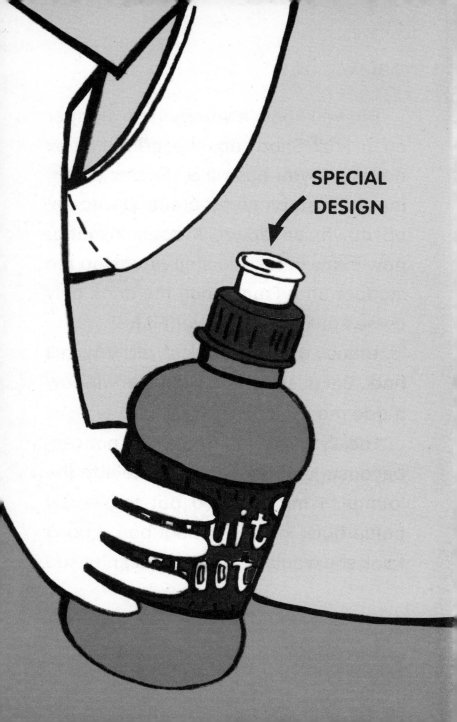

Did you know if you pull the stopper on a Fruit Shoot up, the drink comes out! But if you push the stopper down, the drink stops coming out! Up down, up down, up down, it doesn't matter how many times you stop or unstop the stopper on a Fruit Shoot, the drink only comes out when you want it to!!

Unless you've drunk it all. Which I had. Because waiting by the window made me really thirsty.

Luckily my mum never noticed, because just before she came into the lounge, I managed to put the empty bottle back into my school bag. I don't think she would have been very pleased if she knew I'd drunk all my drink before I'd even left the house!

Before I did leave my house my mum gave me a massive hug and told me to have a lovely, lovely time in London.

Then she told me to stay close to Nanny and Grampy at all times.

Then she told me to listen closely to everything Nanny and Grampy said.

Then she told me to do everything that Nanny and Grampy asked.

And then . . . you'll never guess the next then . . . the next then was . . . she gave me a two-pound coin to spend in London all on myself!

I couldn't believe it! Not only was I going into actual, actual London for a whole day with my nanny and grampy, I was rich too!

I didn't tell Nanny and Grampy about the two pounds though, in case they asked to borrow some of it. I just put it in my jeans pocket, got into the car and did my seat belt up. Well, tried to.

The trouble with seat belts is they are really hard to do up, especially if you've got a school bag on your back.

Nanny said it would probably be a good idea if I took my school bag off, put it on the seat beside me and then put it back on when we arrived at the train station.

So I did.

IT WAS SO EXCIII TING!!!!!

CHAPTER 4

The trouble with arriving at a train station is you can't just go straight to the ticket office and buy your tickets. First you have to find a place to park your car.

Grampy said we should have gone for the 9.18 train, because when we got to the train station car park it wasn't just busy, it was rammed! Honestly, there were cars parked absolutely everywhere! Some people had even parked on the grass!

Nanny said we mustn't park on the grass because if we did we might get a parking ticket. Luckily, we found a really small space between two cars right at the very far end of the car park. Grampy just about managed to squeeze us in.

The trouble with just about managing to squeeze in is it didn't leave us any room to squeeze out.

I couldn't get out of the car, Nanny couldn't get out of the car and Grampy couldn't get out either, because the cars on either side of us were too close. For a moment I thought we were going to have to spend the whole day in the car park instead of London, but luckily Grampy is a really good driver.

He managed to drive the car back out, let me and Nanny get out of the car, and then squeeze the car back in, only a bit more over to one side so that he could just about open his door enough to squeeze himself out eventually too.

Only then I remembered I'd left my school bag on the back seat.

The trouble with leaving my school bag on the back seat is it meant Grampy now had to squeeze himself back between the cars, then squeeze himself back inside his car, reach over

to the back seat, get my school bag, then squeeze himself and my school bag out of the car and back between the two cars again.

Only then he remembered he needed to buy a parking ticket.

The trouble with having to buy a parking ticket is not only do you absolutely have to buy one (because it's the law), you also have to put it on the window ledge inside your car so if traffic wardens come round they

can see you've actually bought one. (Otherwise you get fined.)

Which meant that after squeezing in and out about three times, Grampy now had to walk all the way over to the other side of the car park, find a pay-and-display ticket machine, buy a ticket, walk all the way back to the car, squeeze himself back between the cars, then squeeze himself back inside his car, put the ticket in front of the steering wheel, and then squeeze himself all the way back out of the car all over again.

I think he was a bit worn out by the time we got to the ticket office.

I wasn't. I was really excited! After all, our car was parked, our parking ticket was displayed and now we were about to buy the three most super-exciting train tickets anyone could ever buy!

CHAPTER 5

"Three travel cards to London please.
One child, two adults," Nanny said!

As soon as the lady behind the glass had given Nanny our tickets, I asked if I could keep mine in my pocket. Nanny said that I could so long as I promised not to lose it.

Not losing your ticket is really important because not only did our tickets let us travel on the train all the way into London, they would also allow us to go on all the Tube trains we needed to go on when we were in London too. Without paying any more money!

I one hundred per cent promised not to lose my ticket, and then I put it in the same pocket as my two pound coin. Not for very long though, because guess what the train station sold apart from train tickets?

FRUIT SHOOTS!

As soon as I saw the Fruit Shoots in the train station café, I just had to buy one straight away.

Nanny and Grampy were almost on the platform before they realized I wasn't with them. By the time they saw I was in the café, I'd already bought a Fruit Shoot! With my own money!

It wasn't a blackcurrant one either. It was Apple and Pear!

The trouble with Apple and Pear Fruit Shoots is if you haven't had one before, it makes you really thirsty.

So I unstopped my stopper as quickly as I could.

Nanny said she was surprised my mum hadn't given me a drink to bring with my sandwiches. I didn't mention my empty bottle of blackcurrant.

As soon as we left the café I put my Fruit Shoot straight back into my bag. I mean, I was about to see my very first train platform for the very first time ever and I didn't want to miss a thing!

TRAIN PLATFORMS ARE SOOOOOOO EXCITING!!

The first thing I noticed was there wasn't just one way down to the platform – there were two! One way down had steps and the other way down had a really long slope. Grampy said the really long slope was for people with pushchairs and wheelchairs, but I reckoned it would be just as good for children with skateboards and scooters!

Nanny and Grampy went down to the platform on the steps because they said the exercise would do them good. I didn't.

SLOPES ARE SO MUCH FUN!

Once I'd run all the way down the slope, then all the way back up, then all the way back down, then all the way back up, then all the way back down, then all the way back up, then all the way back down, I ended up on – wait for it . . .

THE ACTUAL PLATFORM ITSELF!!

Actual train platforms are amazing. They stretch a really, really long way in one direction and a really, really long way in the other. They've got places where people can stand and places where people can sit. They've got announcements telling you where the next train is going, what time it's going to arrive and how many stops the train is going to make.

Plus they've got a yellow line all the way along the edge.

Nanny said that it was very important to stay behind the yellow line until our train arrived. When I got closer to the yellow line and looked down I could

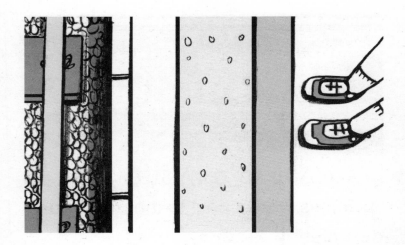

see why!

Guess what you could fall down on to if you stepped over a yellow line on a train platform?

THE ACTUAL TRAIN TRACK!

Guess how far you'd fall?

ABOUT TWO METRES!

Guess what train tracks are made of?

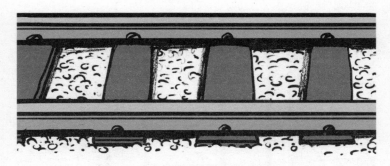

REALLY HARD, DIRTY STEEL!

Guess what's next to the really hard, dirty steel?

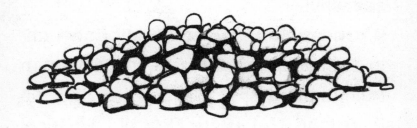

REALLY HARD, DIRTY STONES!

Guess what there is in between the really hard, dirty stones?

REALLY HARD, DIRTY WOOD!

I wouldn't want to fall down on to that!

Grampy said that train tracks keep a train running in a straight line and the wires above give trains their electrical power. I'd hardly even noticed the wires above the train track as I was too busy looking down at the yellow line!

Nanny said the most important part of a train station was definitely the yellow line on the platform, because if we stayed behind it until our train arrived, it would definitely keep us safe.

As soon as I realized how important it was to stay behind the yellow line on a train platform, I started looking at everyone's feet. Most people on our platform were definitely standing behind the yellow line but one man standing quite near to me definitely wasn't. His feet were W A A A A A A A A A Y O V E R the yellow line!

So I tapped him on the back.

The trouble with tapping someone on the back is if you don't do it hard enough they won't feel you tap.

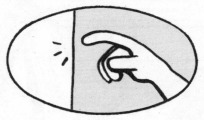

So I tapped him harder.

Only he didn't feel me tap that time either.

So I had to do it again.

When he turned round and looked at me, I told him that he was meant to be standing behind the yellow line.

Trouble is, he was wearing earphones.

The trouble with wearing earphones
is if someone is giving you an important
message you won't be able to hear it.

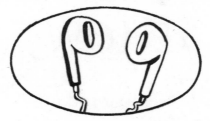

So I shouted at him really loudly.

"YOU'RE MEANT TO STAND BEHIND THE YELLOW LINE!" I hollered.

I think Nanny and Grampy were a bit embarrassed when I shouted. I definitely made them jump. In fact, I think I made everyone on the whole entire platform jump, including the people right down at the very end!

The man with the earphones definitely heard me, because he got back behind the yellow line straightaway. So did everyone else on the platform. Which is a really good job actually, because guess what happened next?

Close your eyes, cover your ears . . .!

A FREIGHT TRAIN CAME THROUGH!!

The trouble with freight trains coming through is if you've never seen a freight train come through you don't know what to expect.

Grampy told me that freight trains don't carry people – they carry ice cream, which means they can't stop at stations because they are in a real hurry to get to London before the ice cream melts.

"STAND BACK FROM THE PLATFORM EDGE. FREIGHT TRAIN APPROACHING!" said the train station announcer. Which was a bit unnecessary really, because I'd already got everyone to stand back from the platform edge. In a much louder voice, too.

When Nanny heard the announcement, she pulled me even further back from the yellow line. And she put her hands over my ears.

I wasn't sure why at first, but then I found out! Because do you know how fast freight trains go?

Very VERY VERY VERY VERY FAST!

Fast enough to make your tummy go whoomph, your whole body shake, your hair go everywhere, your nose scrunch up and both your eyes shut tight!

I wonder what flavour ice cream went through?

CHAPTER 6

I don't know if ice cream gets excited when it goes into London, but when I saw our train arriving at our platform,

I NEARLY BURST!

Grampy told me to wave to the driver as the train came into our station, so I did! The train driver was sitting behind the window at the very front of the train and guess what? WHEN HE SAW ME WAVING TO HIM, HE WAVED BACK! I think he was really excited about going into London too!

As soon as I realized that people on trains to London like waving back, I waved at every single window that went past me, right up until the time the train had stopped. And guess what? LOADS OF DIFFERENT PEOPLE WAVED BACK AT ME TOO!

LONDON TRAINS ARE THE BEST!

When the train doors opened, some people got on very quickly, then more people got on quite quickly, and then Nanny and Grampy got on quite slowly.

Trouble is, when the train doors closed, I was still on the platform.

Because I hadn't decided which end of the train I wanted to sit.

The trouble with deciding which end of a London train to sit is there are two completely different ends to choose from. I mean, if you sit right at the very front of a London train, you'll

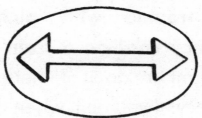

get to London quicker BUT when you get off the train, you won't get to see any of the platform or train that's behind you.

Whereas if you sit right at the back of a London train, you'll get into London slower BUT when you get off you'll get to walk right along the entire length of the platform and count the carriages as you go!

Front of the train? Back of the train? I just couldn't decide.

So Nanny pulled the emergency cord.

The trouble with pulling the emergency cord on a train is you're only meant to do it if there's a real emergency. If you do it when there isn't

a real emergency you can be fined up

to a thousand pounds! Which is even more than a parking ticket, I think?

I didn't know Nanny had pulled the emergency cord inside our train because I was outside on the platform. I did hear the train make a kind of strange funny hissing noise, but when I looked round I couldn't see a real emergency anywhere. I think Grampy was trying to tell me about it through the train door window but I couldn't hear what he was saying through the glass.

It was only when the driver climbed down from the front of the train and walked down the platform to talk to me that I realized the real emergency was me!

When he saw that I was the same person who had waved to him from the platform, he told me not to worry and opened the train doors with his special key. I wasn't actually worried, by the way, I was actually quite excited. I'd never been a real emergency before!

As soon as the doors opened, Nanny grabbed me, pulled me inside the train and gave me the biggest hug ever, which was bit embarrassing really because we'd already done a hug outside my house (plus everyone inside the train was looking at us).

Nanny said sorry to the driver about a hundred times, then said if she hadn't pulled the emergency cord the train would have gone into London and left me behind on the platform.

Which, when I thought about it, was actually true and definitely, definitely, definitely a real emergency!!!

The train driver said he completely understood, but it would take about twenty minutes to get the train to work again. (That's what emergency cords do when you pull them: they totally, totally, totally stop the train from moving.)

Which was quite handy really, because it gave me twenty more minutes to decide which end of the train to sit.

In the end I decided to sit in the middle of the train. Which is a real coincidence, because the middle of the train is exactly where my nanny and grampy had got on in the first place!

How funny is that!

(By the way, in case you are wondering, the train driver didn't fine my Nanny and Grampy a thousand pounds. He decided to let them off. I reckon it was because I was his friend. Thank goodness I'd waved to him!)

CHAPTER 7

Being inside the actual carriage of an actual train going into actual London was amazing. Even if our train hadn't actually started moving yet.

Inside our carriage there was a really long bit in the middle where you can walk up and down. On either side there were rows and rows of seats with really nice stripy material; there were windows you could look out of; there were really high-up places you could put your luggage, plus there were even really low-down rubbish bins with flippy lids!

Our train had absolutely everything that we could ever wish for!

Apart from three seats together.

The trouble with getting three seats together is people who get on a train first get the first choice of all the best seats, whereas people who get on last only get to choose from the seats that are left over.

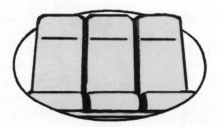

Nanny said that she didn't mind sitting opposite me, and Grampy said he didn't mind sitting opposite Nanny, but I definitely wanted to sit next to Nanny and Grampy, and I definitely

wanted to sit by a window too.
So I asked someone to move.

The trouble with asking someone to move is it's difficult to get their attention if they are reading a newspaper. Especially if they are holding the newspaper up really high.

When I pulled the newspaper down I got such a surprise. So did the man who was reading it, because guess who he was? IT WAS THE SAME MAN WHO HAD HIS FEET ALL OVER THE YELLOW LINE ON THE PLATFORM!

No wonder he didn't hear me when I asked him to move. Not only was he reading a newspaper, he had his earphones in again, too! Well, he did until I pulled them out.

Once I'd got his ears working again I whispered to him very quietly and told him that I needed three seats together. Because my nanny and grampy are really old.

I think he was a bit embarrassed that he hadn't realized we needed his seat. He definitely gave us three seats together, though. In fact, guess what?

HE GAVE US FOUR!

The moment I sat down by the window the train started to move. At last! We were on our way to actual, actual, actual, actual, actual, actual London!

Sitting by the window on a train to

London is totally brilliant, because you get to see things you'd never ever see if you were looking through your window at home.

Did you know that when you're on a train you get to see houses from the other way around? I'd never seen so many back doors and back windows and back gardens in my life!

And did you know that sheep in fields aren't only white? Sometimes they have red or blue splodges on them too.

Plus do you know the most popular name for a sheep is?

Baaaaaaaaarbara.

Grampy told me that too.

Plus did you know that people in London really like drawing? Not on paper though:

on buildings!

And bridges,

and walls

and even on stations!

The closer we got to London, the more drawings I saw.

I saw all sorts of things through the train window on my way into London. I saw houses and offices and churches and schools and traffic jams and building sites and cranes and factories and trees and fields and country lanes and electricity pylons and rivers and lakes and more fields and more sheep. I even saw . . . wait for it . . . an actual sewage works! And a mouldy caravan parked in a field!

Nanny said the caravan wasn't parked, it was abandoned. Which means no one wants to live in it. I'd love to live in a mouldy caravan. Me and Gabby could turn it into a den. (Once my mum had cleaned all the mould off.)

Every time our train stopped at another station, more and more people got on. Which is a bit of a shame really, because by the time we were about halfway to London, I decided I wanted to move seats to the other side of the train so I could look through the window on that side too.

Nanny said it was probably best if we stayed where we were because there weren't any seats left on the train at all, let alone three seats together!

I said I didn't mind asking three more people to move, but Grampy said he'd rather I didn't do that.

So I got my Fruit Shoot out instead.

The trouble with drinking a Fruit Shoot on a train to London is it makes you want to go to the loo.

Especially if you've already drunk a whole Blackcurrant Fruit Shoot, plus a bit of Apple and Pear Fruit Shoot before you've even got on. Double especially if you see a sign pointing to the toilets!

If I hadn't seen the sign pointing to

the toilets, I would never have known that toilets on trains even existed! Nanny asked me if I could cross my legs and hold on until we got to London. But I couldn't. Because I was busting.

So Grampy said he would take me to the toilet on the train.

The trouble with being taken to a toilet on a train is our train was really crowded.

I lost count of the times Grampy had to say "excuse me" while we were trying to squeeze down the middle. Luckily we only had to squeeze through two carriages to get there.

When I saw the toilet on the train I nearly fainted! It was like a space toilet! It had shiny white walls, a not-quite-as-shiny grey floor and big yellow buttons!

I T W A S TOILET-TASTIC!
! ! ! ! ! ! ! ! ! ! ! !

Once Grampy had showed me how all the buttons worked, I couldn't wait to give it a go!

SO (in case you ever go on a train to actual London) THIS IS WHAT YOU NEED TO DO IF YOU WANT TO GO TO THE LOO:

First: Push the big yellow button that says OPEN. (When you do that the door will slide open without you even touching it! Believe me, it's true!)

Second: Step inside, turn around and push the big yellow button that says CLOSE. (When you do that the door will slide closed without you even touching it too! How amazing is that!)

Third: Lock the door by pushing the big yellow button that says LOCK. (When you do that it means no one can walk in by mistake!)

Fourth: Turn around, pull funny faces and jump up and down in front of the mirror. (The mirror is massive, which means however high or wide you jump you can still see your face!)

Fifth: Go to the loo.

Sixth: Wash your hands about eight times. (Because the squirty soap is brilliant fun and the automatic water squirters are totally awesome too!)

Seventh: Dry your hands for ages under the automatic hand drier. (If the air runs out, just wave your hands about until the air starts coming out again.)

Eighth: Wet your hands again with the automatic water squirter and then try out the paper towels too.

(The paper towels are hidden inside a kind of really cool letter box. See if you can pull more than three out in one go!)

Ninth: Pretend you've brought a dolly with you and you need

to change its nappy. (Toilets on trains have a special fold-down shelf for nappy changing too! If you don't like dollies, pretend it's a teddy.)

Tenth: Do loads more silly things in front of the mirror.

Eleventh: Wave to yourself at the end.

Twelfth: Push the big yellow button that says OPEN.

Thirteenth: Go back to your seat.

All the time I was in the toilet Grampy had been knocking on the door to check if I was all right. I kept telling him I was, but I don't think he actually believed me till the door finally opened.

Do you know how long he said I had been in the toilet? TWENTY MINUTES! How crazy is that? To me it only felt like about twenty seconds!

As soon as I saw him, I told him that toilets on trains to London are absolutely amazing and that he should definitely go to the loo too. But Grampy said there wasn't time, because not only did we have to squeeze ourselves all the way down the middle of two carriages back to Nanny, I had to put my Fruit Shoot bottle back in my school bag, put my school bag back on, and get ready to get off the train.

Because guess what?

Wait for it . . .!

That's right . . .!

OUR TRAIN WAS ACTUALLY ARRIVING IN ACTUAL LONDON!!!

When I looked through the window, I could tell our train was arriving in London because not only were the train wheels slowing down a lot, there were drawings absolutely everywhere! There were drawings on the walls beside the train tracks; there were drawings on the walls inside the tunnels; there were drawings on metal posts; drawings on wooden doors – someone had even drawn drawings on top of some drawings!

I think London should buy itself some paper to draw on instead. Or at least get some better felt tips or crayons.

CHAPTER 8

Stepping down on to a London train station platform was amazing! You should have seen how high the station ceiling was!

You should have seen how big the station was! I couldn't really see how long the platform was because there were so many people in the way; there were people in front of us, people behind us and people overtaking us, too. Everyone was in such a hurry to get to the next exciting bit of their journey . . .

THE TICKET BARRIER!

The trouble with ticket barriers is I'd never put a ticket in a ticket barrier before, so when we got to the end of the platform I didn't really know what to do. Grampy told me to have my ticket ready and just follow him and Nanny.

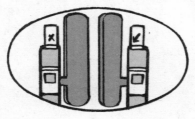

First of all I watched Grampy put his ticket through the ticket barrier, then I watched Nanny put her ticket through the ticket barrier. By the time it was my go I was a total expert.

Putting a ticket through a ticket barrier is one of the whizziest things you can do. Honestly, one moment I was poking my ticket into a hole at the front, the next it was poking out of a hole at the top!

I couldn't believe how fast my ticket whizzed through!

ticket whizzes out here!

ticket goes in here

So I did it again.

And again!

And again and again and again and again!!!!

After I'd whizzed my ticket through the barrier about seven times, Grampy said I really needed to walk through the barrier, because people behind me wanted to put their tickets in too.

When I turned around to have a look, I couldn't believe how many people were standing behind me! Even one of the train station guards had come to see how good I was at whizzing!

Everyone was sooo jealous!!

So I showed them all how to do it a couple of more times, put my ticket back in my pocket and joined Nanny and Grampy on the other side of the barrier.

The main bit of the London train station was MASSIVE! The announcement board was longer than my back garden! There were shops people could shop in, seats people could sit on, ticket machines people could buy tickets from, there were announcements all over the place – plus at least ten other platforms with ticket barriers too!

Grampy said that we were standing in one of the busiest train stations in the whole entire country. He said thousands and thousands of people go through the station every day! I'm not surprised either – it was brilliant!

As soon as we started walking,

Nanny took hold of my hand. Because guess where we were going next . . .?

Over to the other side of the main bit of the station . . .

Down

       some

            steps . . .

All the way up over to . . .

Wait for it . . .

ANOTHER TICKET BARRIER!

Nanny and Grampy didn't tell me we were going to another ticket barrier. I was so surprised when I saw it, I nearly dropped my ticket when I took it out of my pocket!

I couldn't wait to get whizzing again!

Trouble is, Nanny and Grampy said that this time I was only allowed to put my ticket through once.

The trouble with only putting your ticket through once is you only get one whizz.

I wanted to do at least three whizzes, but Nanny said we needed to keep going because we had lots of exciting places to visit.

And she was right, because guess what we visited next . . . just around the corner from the ticket barrier was . . .

Wait for it . . .

Wait for it . . .

You're never going to believe it . . .

AN ESCALATOR!

Escalators are the best stairs on earth, because guess what! THEY MOVE ALL BY THEMSELVES!

The trouble with normal stairs is they don't move at all. You have to do all the hard work yourself.

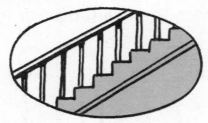

Like, if I was at home and I wanted to get from my bedroom down to my front door, when I got to the stairs I would have to bend my legs on to every single step all the way down to the bottom. Or if I was at home and I wanted to get from my front door up to my bedroom, when I got to the stairs I would have to bend my legs on to every single step of my stairs all the way up to the top.

Which is really tiring.

Escalators aren't tiring at all! Because all you have to do is get on!

When I saw the escalator that me, Nanny and Grampy were about to step on to

I COULDN'T BELIEVE MY EYEBALLS!!!!!

Guess how far it went down . . .!

It went down
and down
and down
and down
and down
and down
and down
and down
and down
and down
and down
and down
and down
and down
and down
and down!!!!!!!!!!!!!!!!!!!!!!!!!!!!!!!!!!!!

Much further than escalators do in the shops!

When Nanny saw how steep the escalator was, she decided to stand in front of me. So did Grampy. So Nanny got on first, Grampy got on second and then I got on third.

The trouble with getting on third is I didn't have a very good view of going down, because all I could see in front of me was Grampy's shirt!

So I moved over to the left.

The trouble with moving over to the left is you're only allowed to stand on the left if, you're in a hurry and want to walk down.

I wasn't in a hurry, and there was no way I was going to walk down that many steps! So I had to move back over to the right. Which meant by the time I got to the bottom of the down escalator, I'd hardly seen anything at all.

Luckily there was an up escalator too!

As soon as Nanny and Grampy turned round and saw me on the up escalator I gave them a really big wave. They didn't wave back, but Grampy thought it was such a good idea he followed me up the up escalator too! Which was really fun, because by the time he was halfway up the up escalator I was halfway down the down escalator again!

Going down the down escalator was much better the second time around, because there was nobody in my way. This time I got to see every single step, I could easily wave to Grampy on my right plus Nanny, who was still waiting for me at the bottom!

As soon as I got off at the bottom, I asked Nanny if she wanted to have a go on the up escalator too, but she said she couldn't, because Grampy had caught up with us again and we had somewhere even more exciting to go . . .!

Can you guess where?

You've guessed it . . .!

THE TUBE!

CHAPTER 9

In case you didn't know, Tube is short for Tube train.

Tube trains aren't short at all, though; they stretch from one end of a Tube station platform all the way to the other end!

Do you know what the long name for Tube train is?

THE LONDON UNDERGROUND.

Do you know why it's called the London Underground? Because it's in London and it goes underground. Honestly, the platforms are under the ground, the train tracks are under the ground, the tunnels are under the ground – plus all Tube trains go under the ground too.

That's why London Underground escalators go so far down. Because escalators are the steepest stairs on earth.

When we got from the escalators to the platform, Nanny showed me the most important part of the whole entire London Underground. That's right – Tube station platforms have yellow danger lines drawn on them too! Only they use a much thinner paintbrush. And they paint them much closer to the edge.

When I asked Grampy which tunnel our Tube train was going to come out of he dared me to guess. And guess what! I GUESSED RIGHT!

I mean left.

I mean I guessed left and left was right!

When our Tube train came out of the tunnel, even my hair got excited. Tube trains have got a window at the front, so the driver can see out (only he didn't wave back) and windows all the way down the side for people to look out of too (only they didn't wave back either.)

Grampy said that people on trains in London aren't as friendly as people on other trains. I still couldn't wait to get on it though.

The trouble with getting on a Tube train is you're not allowed to just get on. First you have to wait for the train to

stop, then you have to wait for the doors to open, then you have to wait for any people inside to get off and THEN you can get on.

It was all right though, because once
we did get on, there were three seats
together EVERYWHERE!

Being inside an actual Tube train was amazing! I could see right down inside the carriages for miles!

And there was loads to see, too!

Guess which way the seats go on a Tube train? SIDEWAYS!

Guess what some of the seats do on a Tube train? FLIP UP AND DOWN!

When I saw someone flip a seat up and down I just had to have a go myself. Only after about ten flips Nanny asked me to sit still for a while.

Sitting still was actually quite exciting too, because it gave me a really good chance to look round.

Guess what colour the metal poles

were inside our Tube train?

RED!

(Metal poles are there for you to hold on to if there aren't any seats to sit on.)

Guess what colour the high-up hand straps were in our Tube train?

RED TOO!

(High-up straps are there for you to hold on to if there aren't any metal poles to hold.)

Guess what colour the windows go when you're going through a tunnel?

BLACK!

Guess what colour the windows go when you arrive at another Tube station?

SEE THROUGH!

And guess what obstructing the doors can be . . .?

DANGEROUS!!!!

As soon as I read the sign that said OBSTRUCTING THE DOORS CAN BE DANGEROUS, I went back to sit with Nanny and Grampy. Because I wanted to find out what "obstructing the doors" actually meant.

Nanny said that when a Tube train gets full up with people, other people still try and get on. Which means when the train driver tries to close the doors there are bits of people in the way.

Grampy said that King Henry the Eighth used to use Tube train doors to chop people's heads off but Nanny told him off for telling fibs. Then she showed me a Tube map to stop me thinking about chopped-off heads.

The trouble with Tube maps is they look like coloured spaghetti. They've got different-coloured lines going absolutely everywhere!

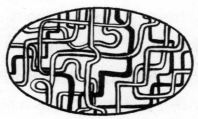

Do you know how many different-coloured lines there are on a Tube map? ELEVEN. Because I counted them.

Do you know how many Tube stations

there are on the London Underground?

Neither do I. Because there are far too many to count.

Nanny told me we were on the red line and that we were going to get off at Oxford Circus. Which made me get really excited, because I thought there were going to be clowns. Only Nanny explained there wouldn't be any clowns at Oxford Circus, or tightrope walkers, or trapeze artists. Oxford Circus is just a very silly name for a Tube station that isn't in Oxford and doesn't have a circus.

Two stops from Oxford Circus, I started thinking about chopped-off heads again, because someone tried to get on to the train when the train doors were closing. Luckily it was only his bag that got chopped.

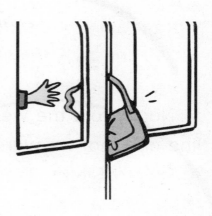

Nanny told me to look away, but I didn't have to because I was already looking away anyway. Not because I was frightened or anything, but because something far more exciting was happening at the other end of our carriage.

Something so exciting, my eyeballs nearly popped out of my face!

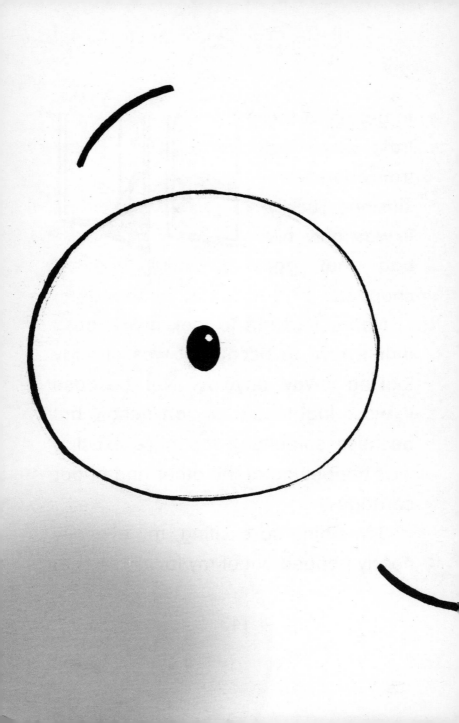

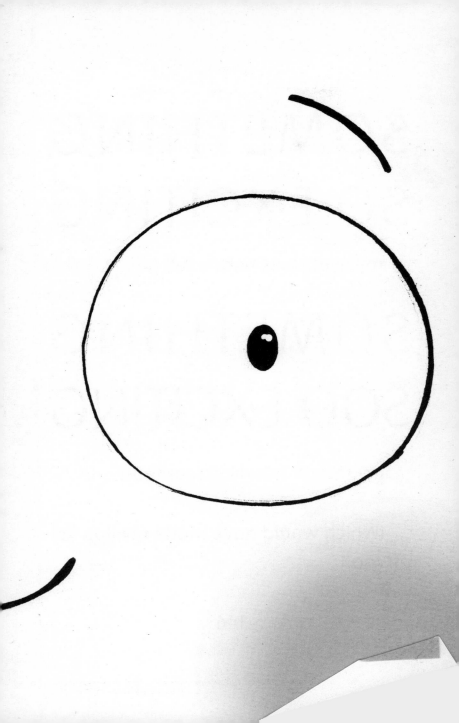

SOMETHING SO EXCITING

my eyebrows nearly fell off!

SOMETHING SOO EXCITING

my mouth nearly screamed!!

(Which would have made my lips fall off too.)

146

Because two stops from Oxford Circus, someone really special got on our train!

Guess who it was . . .?

Go on, have a guess . . .

You'll never guess.

Go on, have another guess.

You'll still never guess.

I couldn't believe it.

I still can't believe it.

BUT IT'S ABSOLUTELY TRUE!!!!!

Ok, I'll tell you . . . it was . . .

A PIGEON!

I told you you wouldn't believe it! But it's totally true!!! An actual pigeon, with an actual beak and wings and everything, had got on to the same actual Tube train carriage as us and was walking across the actual floor

STRAIGHT TOWARDS ME! AND DOUBLE GUESS WHAT!!

HE WANTED TO BE MY FRIEND!!!

CHAPTER 10

As soon as I saw Cooey walking towards me (Cooey is the name I decided to call him), I kept really, really still, because I didn't want to frighten him away.

No one else in our carriage kept very still when they saw him though. Some people turned pages on their newspapers; one lady opened a laptop; one man even crossed his legs!

But Cooey still kept walking towards me. Because he really, really, really wanted to be my friend.

Cooey

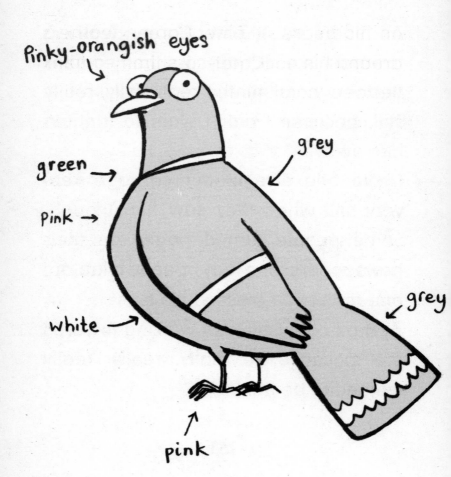

Pinky-orangish eyes

green →

pink →

white →

grey

grey

pink

Cooey was really lovely. Some of him was grey, and some of him was white. He had pinky-orangish eyes, a white bit on his beak, shimmery green feathers around his neck, not-so-shimmery pink feathers near his tummy, blackish tips on his wings and pink feet. He was definitely the nicest pigeon I'd ever met. (Actually, he was the only pigeon I'd ever met.)

When Nanny told me that pigeons quite often get on Tube trains, I realized it was OK to move more than just my eyeballs.

"Do they need to buy a ticket?" I asked her.

"Only at *beak* times," said Grampy.

The closer Cooey got to me, the more I started to realize how hungry he was. When he started pecking at the floor of the Tube train I realized he was actually STARVING!

Luckily, I had my sandwiches in my school bag.

The trouble with having sandwiches in your school bag is sometimes they can be really hard to reach.

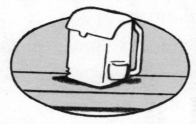

Especially if you don't want your nanny and grampy to see what you're doing.

Double especially if your nanny is sitting right next to you!

So I had to do everything left-handed. **The trouble with doing everything left-handed** is I'm right-handed.

Which means my left fingers are my least best fingers to use.

First, I had to slowly move my left arm over to my bag.

Then I had to sloowly use all my wrong fingers to unzip the zip.

Then I had to slooowly put my arm

inside my bag.

Then slooooowly reach down inside.

Then slooooowly use my wrong fingers again to pull the lid off my sandwich box.

Then sloooooowly pull some crumbs off one of my sandwiches.

Then slooooooooooooooooooooowly lift my crumbs out of my bag, slooooooooooooooooooooooooooooowly slide my hand down besides my knee and quickly drop them on to the floor.

As soon as Cooey saw my crumbs he came right up to my shoe and gobbled up every single bit!

So I did it again. And again. And again.

Because he was definitely still hungry. In fact he was really, really starving.

By the time we arrived at the next platform, I had tried him on breadcrumbs

and bread crust,

I even gave him a piece of my cheese!

But then I had to stop, because the train doors were opening.

The trouble with train doors opening is it meant people inside our train wanted to get off

The other trouble with train doors opening is the people outside our train wanted to get on.

I didn't want anyone to get on or off; I just wanted everyone to stay really still.

But they didn't. No one stayed still at all.

Which meant Cooey got really frightened.

And jumpy.

And flappy.

When Cooey jumped up into the air and started flapping, the people getting on and off the train didn't know what to do. One man ducked down, another man waved his newspaper, one lady dropped her handbag and another lady even screamed! No one even thought of giving him something to eat.

No wonder Cooey got off without saying goodbye.

He'd have got totally squashed if he hadn't, and I wouldn't have wanted that to happen.

I still really missed him, though. And I was sure he'd be missing me.

CHAPTER 11

Once our train started moving again, all I could think about was Cooey. I still had loads of my sandwich left in my bag, but now I had no one I could feed it to.

When the doors opened at Oxford Circus, I was hoping Cooey would be waiting for me on the platform, but there were so many people there, I think they probably frightened him away.

Luckily Nanny cheered me up because guess where she told me we were going next . . . Go on, guess. OK, I'll tell you . . .

A COMPLETELY DIFFERENT
PLATFORM TO CATCH A
COMPLETELY DIFFERENT TUBE
TRAIN ON A COMPLETELY
DIFFERENT LINE!

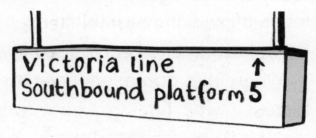

victoria line ↑
Southbound platform 5

When I found out we were going to go to a completely different platform to catch a completely different Tube train on a completely different line, I got really excited again.

Until I saw the normal steps.

The trouble with normal steps is they don't escalate – especially short sets of steps.

I wanted to escalate all the way to our next platform, only this time I had to lift my legs and everything.

Grampy said that the London Underground doesn't have short escalators, especially short escalators that go around corners. Which made me realize that there was another load of steps hidden around the corner of the steps I was already climbing!

And I was right.

As far as I'm concerned

NORMAL SHORT STEPS
  + MORE NORMAL SHORT STEPS
    = LONG NORMAL STEPS.

So by the time we got to the next platform, I was absolutely exhausted.

Luckily, an old lady stood up and gave me her seat.

When I saw our next train arriving, I got my energy back straight away. Which was a good job, because when we got inside the train, it was so crowded I had to stand up! Even Grampy and Nanny had to stand!

It's a good job I'm really good at standing. And balancing, otherwise I would definitely have fallen over.

Guess what colour the hand straps were inside the Tube?

BLUE.

Guess who was too short to reach them?

ME.

Guess what colour the metal poles were on our Tube?

BLUE TOO.

Guess who was too squashed in to reach them.

ME!

Luckily we only had to go one stop.

CHAPTER 12

When we got off the Tube train at Green Park Tube station, guess what we got to go on next . . .?

ANOTHER ESCALATOR GOING UP!

And up and up and up and up!

Escalating up the up escalator at Green Park Tube station was a hundred times better than walking up two loads of steps at Oxford Circus.

Halfway up the escalator, the wind really started to blow too, which made it even more fun! Well, it did for me; not so much for Nanny's new hairdo.

At the very, very top of the escalator things got even better than better, because not only was our hair still blowing all over the place, there was . . .

Wait for it . . .

ANOTHER TICKET BARRIER!

As soon as I saw we had another ticket barrier to go through, I got my ticket totally ready! Trouble is, Grampy only let me whizz it through once, because there were lots of people behind us getting off at Green Park too.

I still did a really good whizz though!

If you ask me, Green Park is a much better name for a Tube station than Oxford Circus. Because when you get outside into the sunshine, not only is there a park – the park is green.

You should have seen the size of the trees in Green Park! They were

TREENORMOUS!

When I saw them, I started looking for Cooey again. Because I was sure he'd be looking for me, too.

Trouble is, I couldn't see him anywhere. All I could see were people. There were people walking in front of us, people walking behind us, people were walking on the grass, sitting on the grass, lying on the grass, one lady was even doing really slow karate on the grass!

There was no way that I would have

been able to see Cooey and no way that Cooey would have been able to see me.

So I decided to leave him a trail of crumbs to follow.

And cheese.

And ham.

And ham.

The trouble with leaving Cooey a trail of crumbs, cheese, ham and ham is before I could do it, I had to get Nanny and Grampy to let go of my hands. Otherwise I wouldn't be able to get to my sandwiches.

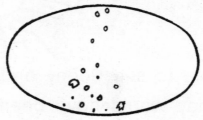

Telling Nanny and Grampy that I was dying of thirst was one of the best ideas I've ever had in my whole entire life. Because not only did it mean we had to

stop on the grass to get my Fruit Shoot
out, it gave me a chance to smuggle
one of my sandwiches out, too. And
hide it under my T-shirt. (Well, half up
my T-shirt, half inside my jeans.)

Leaving a trail for Cooey was easy after that. I'm not sure how many hundreds of crumbs there were in my trail, but it was definitely a whole sandwich's worth.

By the time we got to the end of the path there was still no sign of Cooey though.

Which was a real shame, because guess what I could have shown him if he'd been there . . .?

THE BIGGEST AND POSHEST GATES I'VE EVER SEEN!

When I saw the gates at the end of Green Park, I nearly dropped my Fruit Shoot! Not only was the metal all swirly and pointy and fancy, the poshest bits were painted with. Wait for it . . .

ACTUAL GOLD!

I didn't know you could get paint made from actual gold, but you can in London!

"Welcome to Buckingham Palace!" said Grampy.

CHAPTER 13

Guess who lives inside Buckingham Palace?

THE ACTUAL QUEEN!

Guess what colour the ground is outside Buckingham Palace?

PINK!

Guess who stands really still on the pink bit outside Buckingham Palace?

ACTUAL SOLDIERS!

When I asked Grampy if we could go inside Buckingham Palace and say hello to the Queen, he said that she was having her hair done just like Nanny did.

So we walked to St James's Park instead.

CHAPTER 14

The trouble with walking to St James's Park is I'd already walked from Green Park station to Buckingham Palace.

So I asked if we could get a taxi instead. Nanny said that taxis in London are far too expensive and that it wasn't very far for us to walk. Which was handy really, because guess what I suddenly saw on a triangle bit of pavement just outside Buckingham Palace . . .?

TRAFFIC LIGHT BUTTONS!

I love pressing traffic light buttons! My mum always lets me push the buttons when we're crossing roads at home. Just outside Buckingham Palace there's not one, not two, but THREE different traffic light buttons you can push!!! So I made sure I pushed every single one!!!

Once I'd stopped all the traffic in every single direction, Grampy said it would probably be best if we kept on walking, but I still did one more press of all of them. Just for luck!

Nanny said I'd love St James's because it's got swings, a sand pit and a lake going all the way down the middle. Trouble is, I wasn't looking for swings, a sand pit, or a lake going down the middle. I was looking for Cooey.

When I saw the lake, I hoped it might be the kind of place where Cooey would come to meet me, especially if some of his best friends were ducks. But on the pavement outside there was a sign that shows you drawings of all the birds you can see in St James's Park. Really good drawings too.

The trouble with greylag geese, tawny owls, white pelicans, moorhens, great spotted woodpeckers, blue tits, coots, grey herons, swifts, tufted duck males, tufted duck females, common terns, great crested grebes with chicks, cormorants, pochard males, pochard females, kestrels, black caps and reed warblers

is none of them are **pigeons**.

So we went to Westminster Abbey
instead.

CHAPTER 15

Did you know Westminster Abbey is almost a thousand years old?

It hasn't got any pigeons in it though.

CHAPTER 16

As soon as we came out of Westminster Abbey, I had another drink of my Fruit Shoot because we'd been in there for ages and looking at statues makes me really thirsty.

Nanny said we were going to walk to the Houses of Parliament next and then after that we should think about having our lunch.

The trouble with walking to the Houses of Parliament is I'd already walked from Green Park station to Buckingham Palace to St James's Park and all the way to Westminster Abbey!

So I asked Nanny if we could get a taxi
this time instead.

Nanny said that taxis were still too
expensive and that another short walk
would help us work up an appetite for
lunch. So I had no choice really.

We didn't exactly walk though.

Did you know that when you go past
the Houses of Parliament you have to
walk on tiptoe?

Grampy says that the Houses of Parliament are where MPs go to sleep, so if you're passing you need to make as little noise as possible.

And I believed him too, until we got bonged.

The trouble with bongs is they're really loud. Especially the bongs that come from Big Ben.

BONG!

Big Ben is the most famous clock in the whole of London because its bell does really big bongs. If you stay up late enough you can even hear Big Ben bonging on the news!

There is no way that anyone inside the Houses of Parliament could sleep through a Big Ben bong. Let alone TWO Big Ben bongs!!

If you ask me, Big Ben should definitely be called Big Bong.

By the time we had walked from Green Park Station to Buckingham Palace to St James's Park to Westminster Abbey, tiptoed past the Houses of Parliament and all the way up to Big Bong, my legs were nearly falling off. And my head was melting.

But Nanny and Grampy still wouldn't let me get a taxi.

Nanny said that she knew a really good walking game called 'Count the Statues'. Trouble is, I'd already seen loads of statues in Westminster Abbey, and I didn't want my Fruit Shoot to run out. So we played 'Count The Buses and Telephone Boxes' instead.

Guess what colour London buses are?

RED!

Guess how many London buses I counted?

SEVEN!

Guess what colour London telephone boxes are?

RED TOO!

Guess how many red telephone boxes I saw on the way to 10 Downing Street?

SIX IN A ROW!

Guess how many police officers were standing outside the gates of 10 Downing Street?

THREE!

Guess what they were holding?

ACTUAL GUNS!

Guess who they were guarding?

THE ACTUAL PRIME MINISTER! (We didn't actually get to see anyone though. Maybe they were at the hairdressers too?)

Walking down the roads from Big Bong to lunch was actually a lot less tiring than I thought it was going to be, because not only did I win at counting buses and telephone boxes, I even saw a cowboy policeman riding an actual horse down the middle of the actual road!

Talking of actual roads – I wonder who lives at 10 Upping Street?

CHAPTER 17

If I'd known all along where we were going to go for our lunch, I'd have wanted to skip Green Park, Buckingham Palace, St James's Park, Westminster Abbey, Big Bong and Downing Street and go there STRAIGHT AWAY!

Because guess whereabouts in London Nanny and Grampy took me to eat my sandwiches?

TRAFALGAR SQUARE!

And guess who was there waiting to meet me?

COO

I knew it was Cooey because as soon as I got my sandwich out, he came over to me straight away!

And guess who he brought with him? HIS IDENTICAL BROTHERS! AND HIS IDENTICAL SISTERS!! AND THEIR IDENTICAL FRIENDS! I reckon Cooey must have told every pigeon in London about me, because even his quite similar friends wanted to be my friend too!

When Nanny saw Cooey and his friends flying towards me, she wanted me to shoo them away, because there's

a really mean sign in Trafalgar Square that means DO NOT FEED THE PIGEONS.

If I was the Prime Minister, I'd put a sign in Trafalgar Square that says DO NOT READ THE SIGN THAT SAYS DO NOT FEED THE PIGEONS. Because pigeons have to eat too. Especially if they are starving.

And anyway, I was only going to give them a little bit, because I needed to save some sandwich for my lunch too.

Grampy said that if I wasn't careful I'd get pooed on, but people who are best friends never poo on each other. At least, my BFF Gabby has never pooed on me. And anyway it didn't matter, because I had a rain mac in my bag, so I put that on just in case! Even if it was really sunny!

Cooey and his friends were definitely starving, because as soon as I held out my little bit of sandwich, they all tried to jump on it at the same time! Then before I knew what was happening they were pecking my big bit of sandwich too. Even though I'd hidden it behind my back!

The trouble with having pigeons pecking in front of you and behind you

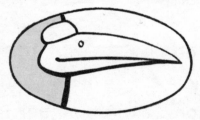

is sometimes their beaks start to miss. Which means sometimes your fingers get pecked instead. Because starving beaks can get really excited.

As soon as my fingers started getting pecked by actual pigeons beaks, I dropped both pieces of my sandwich.

After about a hundred more pecks, every single crumb of my sandwich was totally gone. Which meant the whole entire sandwich my mum had made me for lunch was now completely gone too.

So I pretended to eat air instead.

The trouble with eating air is it's really difficult. Because there's nothing to chew or swallow.

When Nanny noticed I wasn't holding anything in my fingers, she asked me where my lunch was.

When I told her that I didn't have any more sandwiches left in my lunch box, she was really, really surprised. So was Grampy. (I didn't tell them I'd dropped the other half of my sandwich in Green Park.)

216

Grampy said I wasn't to worry and that I could help myself to their sandwiches instead.

So I tried.

The trouble with helping yourself to other people's sandwiches is tuna and cucumber sandwiches aren't cheese, ham and ham. Neither are egg and cress.

So Grampy had to go and find a sandwich shop, because he didn't want me to starve like the pigeons.

While Grampy was gone, Nanny told me all about Trafalgar Square.

Guess who the statue is at the top of Nelson's Column?

NELSON!

Guess who Nelson was?

THE MOST FAMOUS SEA ADMIRAL IN THE WHOLE WIDE WORLD.

Guess how many eyes Nelson had?

ONE!

Guess how many arms he had?

ONE!

Guess how he lost them?

IN ACTUAL BATTLE!

No wonder London gave him such a high statue!

When Grampy came back from the sandwich shop, he gave me a brand-new cheese, ham and ham sandwich, all wrapped up inside a really posh paper bag. Even the sandwich inside the paper bag was wrapped up!

Guess what else he put inside the bag too?

A PACKET OF CHEESY SNIPS!

(I saved those until after my sandwich!)

Honestly, if you like cheese, ham and ham sandwiches you should definitely go to London. London cheese is so much cheesier than normal cheese and London ham is so much hammier. Trouble is before I could even take a bite though, I had to get wet-wiped.

YUK!

The trouble with wet wipes is they are all wet and wipey. (Especially Nanny's wet wipes.)

Nanny didn't just wet-wipe my fingers; she wet-wiped my hands, she wet-wiped my face, she nearly wet-wiped my ears! Then before I could even unwrap the paper on my sandwich she made me promise not to give a single crumb of it to Cooey or his friends.

Luckily I had cheesy snips to give them later so it didn't really matter.

When Cooey and his friends realized I wasn't allowed to share any of my new sandwich with them, they went for a walk somewhere else. There are loads of places you can go in Trafalgar Square if you're a pigeon.

There are four giant statues of the Lion King you can climb on.

If you're not afraid of heights, you can fly all the way up to the top of Nelson's Column and sit on his hat.

If you are afraid of heights, there are lots of steps and lower-down statues you can sit on too. (No hats though.)

If you're thirsty there's even a giant fountain you can dip your beak in!

Trafalgar Square was the perfect place for me to have my lunch, even if the sign does say you're not allowed to feed the pigeons.

As soon as I'd eaten every bit of my new sandwich, I asked if I could go and sit by the edge of the fountain on my own.

Nanny got a bit nervous when I said the word "fountain", and then even more nervous when I said "on my own", but Grampy gave me a wink and told me not to fall in.

As if I would!

Guess what Trafalgar Square fountain is full of? (Apart from water.) ACTUAL MONEY!

People come from all over the world to throw money into the water and make wishes!

Guess what types of statue there are by the edge of Trafalgar Square fountain SPITTING DOLPHINS! PLUS A MERMAID WHO LOOKS LIKE A MAN!

(I don't know what he or she was famous for.)

Lots of people were sitting around the edge of Trafalgar Square fountain. I was the only one with a bag of cheesy snips though! Pigeons love cheesy snips because not only are they really cheesy, the snips have been snipped into all kinds of different shapes.

As soon as I accidentally tipped cheesy snips all over my lap Cooey came back to see me straight away!

Guess what Cooey's favourite shape of cheesy snip is?

TRIANGLE!

Maybe because they're the same shape as his beak.

Guess what Cooey's second favourite shape of cheesy snips is?

HEART-SHAPED!

Definitely because he loves me more than anyone else.

When Cooey's identical brothers, identical sisters and identical-and-quite-similar friends saw me and Cooey sharing cheesy snips, they came charging over to the fountain all at once!

Which made me accidentally tip cheesy snips all over my head and my shoulders too. (Don't worry, I still had my rain mac on!)

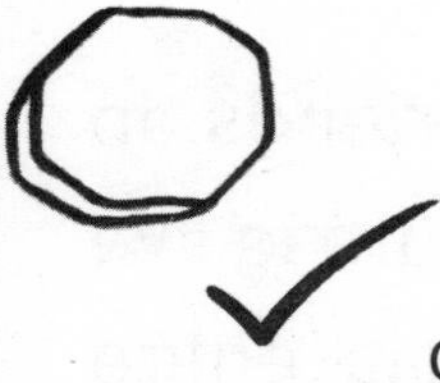

There wasn't
a single shape
of cheesy snip
that Cooey and his friends
didn't like! They liked the moon
shapes and the hexagons 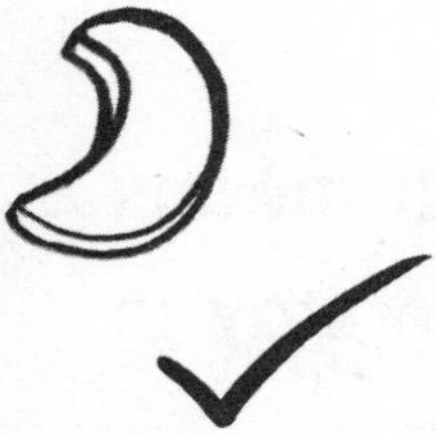
and the rectangles and the
slightly curved
rectangles 
and the ovals
and the diamonds
and the flower shapes
too; they didn't even mind
if some of the
shapes were
broken!

233

Feeding Cooey and his friends in Trafalgar Square was the best thing I've accidentally done in my whole entire life!

Trouble is, just as I was really getting to know them, Nanny and Grampy said it was time for us to go!

The trouble with going is it means you're not staying. I wanted to stay in

Trafalgar Square for the rest of my life, but Nanny and Grampy said that time was getting on and we still had the

Tower of London to see.

When I suggested that they go to the Tower of London and I stay in Trafalgar Square, they said they couldn't go anywhere in London without me.

So I had to go, really. I had to leave Cooey, I had to leave his brothers and his sisters and every single one of his friends in Trafalgar Square, even though they all wanted me to stay too.

Before I waved them goodbye, I told Cooey exactly where I was going next because I really, really wanted him to follow me.

Trouble is, I didn't see him get on our Tube train at Embankment station. Or Temple, or Blackfriars or Mansion

House or Cannon Street or Monument stations either.

Cooey wasn't there at the top of the first normal steps at Tower Hill.

Or the second load of normal steps.

Or the third load of normal steps.

He wasn't there to see me whizz my ticket through the ticket barrier. And he wasn't waiting outside in the sunshine when we got out of Tower Hill station either. I couldn't see Cooey anywhere. All I could see was people, people, people, people, people and more people! Everybody wanted to go to the Tower of London!

Except me. I wanted to be with Cooey.

CHAPTER 18

Guess how many people visit the Tower of London every year?

OVER THREE MILLION. (Grampy looked it up on his phone.)

Guess how many people were standing in the queue to get in?

ABOUT TWO MILLION. (I lost count after fifteen.)

When Nanny saw how long the queue was, she said we probably should have gone to the Tower of London earlier in the day, when it was quieter and not so hot.

Luckily I still had some Fruit Shoot left in my bottle. And I'd taken my rain mac off.

Once we got closer to the front of the queue I started to get quite excited again, because I'd never been inside an actual tower before.

When we finally, finally, finally got to the front of the queue and Nanny asked the lady for three tickets I got really, really excited!

Because guess what kind of tickets Nanny bought us?

SHE BOUGHT US THREE TICKETS TO SEE NOT ONLY THE TOWER OF LONDON BUT . . . WAIT FOR IT . . .

THE CROWN JEWELS TOO!!!!!!

When Grampy told me what the
Crown Jewels actually are, I couldn't
believe my ears.

Guess who the Crown Jewels belong to?

THE ACTUAL QUEEN!

Guess what kind of jewels the Queen has in her crown?

WHOPPING DIAMONDS, MASSIVE EMERALDS, GIANT SAPPHIRES AND ENORMOUS RUBIES!

Guess how much the Crown Jewels are worth?

MILLIONS AND MILLIONS AND MILLIONS AND MILLIONS AND MILLIONS AND MILLIONS AND MILLIONS OF POUNDS!

No wonder they keep them in a tower!

Grampy told me that the Queen

doesn't only have jewels in her crown.
She's got diamond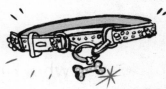
dog collars for her
corgis; she's got a

 TV remote covered in
emeralds; she's got
a ruby rolling pin for

baking cakes and
a sapphire garden
fork for growing
vegetables!

 I absolutely couldn't
wait to see them. Trouble
is, there was a massive
queue to see the Crown
Jewels as well! I couldn't believe it!!!!

When my legs saw the queue for the Crown Jewels they nearly fell off because they were still aching from the queue they'd already queued in.

Nanny said she knew a "really good queuing up to see the Crown Jewels game" called 'How Many Kings and Queens Can We Think Of'. Luckily, a Beefeater came to talk to us instead!

Guess what a Beefeater is?
SOMEONE WHO EATS BEEF!

Guess what a Beefeater does?
GUARDS THE TOWER OF LONDON, INCLUDING THE CROWN JEWELS!

When I saw an actual Beefeater talking to people in our queue, I went straight up to him and asked him to come and talk to us too.

And guess what?
HE DID!

When I told him my name was Daisy, he told me his name was Cyril. Cyril knew absolutely everything there is to know about the Tower of London.

Did you know that in the year 16 something or other, a man called Captain Blood actually stole the Crown Jewels and ran away with them! Before he could sell them though, he was captured and made to give them back.

Even Grampy didn't know that!

When I asked Cyril why he was wearing a dress, he said it wasn't a dress; it was special uniform that only Beefeaters are allowed to wear. It did actually look quite special, because it had a golden crown on the front with the letters E and R on either side too.

Guess what the letters E and R stand for on a Beefeater's uniform?

EARLY RISER. (Because Beefeaters have to get up really early every morning to cook the beef.)

Cyril told me that.

When I asked Cyril if he ate anything else apart from beef, he said no, only beef.

I told him that he should definitely try cheese, ham and ham sandwiches. And cheesy snips.

Cyril said he'd like to, but if he got caught he might get his head chopped off.

Which was definitely a fib. (Nanny told me that.)

Queuing up to see the Crown Jewels was much more fun than queuing up in the first queue we queued in. (Thanks to Cyril.) I might even decide to be a Beefeater one day, when they're allowed to eat other things apart from beef. (Not including peas.)

The closer we got to the front of the Crown Jewels queue, the closer we got to the cannons. That's right. The Crown Jewels are guarded outside by four actual cannons! PLUS two soldiers who are really good at standing still.

Cyril said that if anyone like Captain

Blood ever tries to steal the Crown Jewels again, the really still soldiers will suddenly spring into life and fire cannon balls at them!

Then he told me where they hide their cannon balls!

You'll never guess where. . .

UNDER THEIR HATS!!!

If you ask me, the Crown Jewels building should have a diamond-covered drinks machine for people who nearly die of thirst when they're queuing. The Queen can definitely afford it.

Luckily we didn't have too much longer to wait. When we finally, finally got inside the actual Crown Jewels building it felt much, much cooler. Which was a good job because I had totally run out of Fruit Shoot plus we still had a bit more queuing to do. Trouble is, it wasn't just cooler inside the Crown Jewels building, it was really dark and a bit spooky too.

The trouble with things being really dark and a bit spooky too is it made me want to go back out into the sunshine again. Because sunshine isn't the slightest bit dark or spooky, it's really bright and about as unspooky as you can get.

Leaving the queue for the crown jewels and going back outside into the sunshine was definitely the best thing I could ever have done.

Even if Nanny and Grampy didn't

realize I'd done it.

Because guess who I spotted in the sunshine, over on the grass over by a really tall tree . . .

COOEY!

AND HE WAS LIMPING!

CHAPTER 19

As soon as I saw Cooey limping outside on the grass, I just knew I had to go to him straight away. So I left my school bag on the floor and ran outside to help him. Trouble is, the grass was right over the other side of the Tower by some trees.

When I think about it now, I probably should have told Nanny and Grampy where I was going. But I didn't really have time, because Cooey was in trouble and they wouldn't have wanted to lose their place in the queue.

So I just ran to him as fast as I could.

The trouble with following a limping pigeon is sometimes they don't just limp. Sometimes they hop and fly as well.

First, I followed Cooey over to a big tree. Then I followed him towards a slightly smaller tree. Then he limped across the grass for a bit, then he flew to the end of the grass, then he got frightened by a big crowd of people who weren't looking where they were going. Then he flew over a little metal fence, and limped across some more grass. Then he hopped back over the fence and disappeared for a bit. Then he limped across some pavement, then all the way down a really steep slope. Then I couldn't see where he was limping or flying to because a whole load more people got in the way. Then he suddenly flew up into the air and swooped through the archway at the bottom of the slope. Then he went left and flew all the way to the end of another long wall. Then he hopped round in circles for a bit (I think all the people around him were making him dizzy) then . . . just when I thought I was going to get really close up to him, he flew right up on to the very top of the wall, winked at me and jumped over!

As soon as I saw Cooey do an actual wink at me, I realized exactly what he was doing. He was leading me somewhere special and he wanted me to follow!

I didn't know where he was leading me because pigeons can't speak. But I definitely know he wanted me to follow him.

So I did.

Not over the wall – I went right along to the very end of the wall, turned the corner, kept on walking, stopped at the end, opened my mouth and stared.

Because guess what Cooey was wanting to show me!

THE RAVENS!

Guess what ravens are?
WHOPPING GREAT BIRDS.
Guess how whopping?

ABOUT TWICE AS WHOPPING AS A PIGEON.

Guess what colour ravens are?

BLACK ALL OVER!

(Apart from their bracelets.)

Guess what colour their bracelets are?

PINK!

Guess how many ravens live at the Tower of London?

SEVEN!

Guess what their names are?

MERLINA, JUBILEE, HARRIS, GRIPP, ROCKY, ERIN AND POPPY!

Guess who looks after them?

A different Beefeater called Jeff!

As soon as I saw the raven cage at

the Tower of London, I got really excited because not only was it about four times bigger than my garden shed, it was covered in wire that's completely see through.

That's how I first saw Jeff, because he was inside the cage, sweeping the floor and talking to two of the ravens in actual raven language!

JEFF THE BEEFEATER is a total expert on ravens. In fact, he told me that he doesn't just look after the ravens at the Tower of London: he is the official Ravenmaster!

That's not all he told me either.

According to ancient, olden-day

legend, if six of the ravens ever leave the Tower of London and don't come back, the walls will totally crumble. I'm not sure how though, because if I had wings, I'd have to flap them really hard to even move a brick, let alone crumble one? Even six wings.

I told Jeff that the best way to stop the ravens ever leaving The Tower of London is to keep the door of their cage locked, but he said they are allowed to fly wherever they want, as long as they are home in time for dinner.

When I asked him what ravens eat for dinner, I thought he would say cheesy snips at least. But he didn't. Ravens don't eat anything normal at all.

They eat . . .

Wait for it . . .

Dead mice, dead rats, dead chicks, dead quails, dead red meats, dead white meats, dead biscuits, dead boiled eggs and dead blood!!!!!

Talking to Jeff was so interesting. When I told him that I wanted to be an official Pigeonmaster one day, he said he was sure I would be brilliant at looking after pigeons. Then, just as I was going to ask him if he'd seen Cooey anywhere, he asked me who was actually looking after me.

That's when I remembered that I

should probably be getting back to Nanny and Grampy.

When I told Jeff where my Nanny and Grampy were, he said he was going that way too, so he walked me all the way back to the Crown Jewels building. Which was really nice of him.

When I walked inside, I couldn't wait to tell Nanny and Grampy all about Cooey's limp AND all about the ravens too! Trouble is, they weren't there. Even my school bag wasn't there. Can you believe it! Nanny and Grampy had completely vanished! Without even telling me where they were going! They hadn't even left me a note!

Luckily the ticket-checking people recognized me. In fact they were so pleased to see me, they even did a walkie talkie announcement to one of the other Beefeaters!

And guess which Beefeater it was?

CYRIL!

When Cyril came back with Nanny
and Grampy, Nanny was in a bit of a tizz.

I don't think I've ever seen her face so red. Mind you, it was a really hot day.

Nanny said that she and Grampy had been going around in circles trying to find me. She said they'd looked for me in the White Tower, the Bloody Tower, the Chapel and the gift shop. They'd even looked in the moat!

I told them that they would have been much better off staying in the Crown Jewels Building until I got back, but that only made Nanny go even redder.

When I said I was ready to go in and see the Crown Jewels now, Nanny said that she wasn't capable of taking any more steps in London today and that it was time for us to go back to the train station . . . Wait for it . . .

IN AN ACTUAL TAXI!!!!

Can you believe it! After spending all day telling me that taxis in London are far too expensive, Nanny and Grampy had now completely changed their minds!!!!! I think they just wanted to surprise me!

LONDON TAXIS

CHAPTER 20

On the train home, Grampy told me everything he knew about pigeons. Nanny went to sleep. Well, I think she went to sleep. She definitely kept her eyes shut.

Did you know there are basically two types of pigeon?

Wood pigeons live in woods and eat acorns.

Racing pigeons live in cities and eat anything.

Guess what type of pigeon Cooey looks most like?

A RACING PIGEON!

Guess what racing pigeons are good at doing?

RACING!

Which makes sense actually, because when Cooey first saw my cheese, ham and ham sandwich on the Tube train, he definitely raced to me!

When I asked Grampy why he thought Cooey had been limping, he said he had probably followed me from Trafalgar Square all the way to Embankment Tube station, seen us get on the Tube, tried to hop on just as the train doors were closing and got his ankle squashed in the doors.

Which makes sense actually.

Then he promised me that there was no need for me to worry about Cooey because pigeon limps heal really quickly. Was I pleased to hear that!

When I told Grampy that Cooey was my second BFF after Gabby, he had an even better idea.

So now Gabby is my BFF (BEST FRIEND FOREVER).

And Cooey is my BFFF (BEST FEATHERED FRIEND FOREVER).

It was the perfect end to a perfect trip!

Well, it was until we got home.

CHAPTER 21

Guess what Nanny told my mum as soon as we got indoors! She said I had got lost in the Tower of London!!!!!

I didn't get lost! I knew exactly where I was all the time! First of all I was in the Crown Jewels building, then I was following Cooey with his limp, then I was meeting the ravens, then I was having a really lovely chat with Jeff about him doing his raven mastering and me doing my pigeon mastering, then I was walking back to the Crown Jewels building with Jeff, and then when I got there, Nanny and Grampy were nowhere to be seen! Because they were going around and around in circles getting lost trying to find me. Thank goodness Cyril found them!

Trouble is, before I even got a chance to explain, Grampy completely changed the subject and asked me to tell Mum about all the things I'd done today instead.

When Mum heard about all the barriers I whizzed my ticket through and the escalators I went up and down and the traffic light buttons I pushed, she said no wonder London is the most famous capital city in the world. There are so many interesting things for people to see and do!

And she was right!

After Nanny and Grampy had waved us goodbye I told Mum all about the ravens as well.

And guess what!

My mum has got a pink bracelet too!

I haven't mentioned Cooey yet. Or his identical brothers and sisters, and quite similar friends. Just in case she asks me how I enjoyed the sandwiches she made me!

GULP!

THE END

P.S. If you're wondering what I did with my 80p change, I spent it all on a wish in the Trafalgar Square fountain.

No sign of him yet though!

DAISY'S
TROUBLE INDEX

The trouble with . . .

greylag geese,

 tawny owls,

 white pelicans,

 moorhens,

 great spotted woodpeckers,

 blue tits,

 coots,

 grey herons,

 swifts,

tufted duck males,
 tufted duck females,

 common terns,

 great crested grebes with chicks,

 cormorants,

 pochard males,
 pochard females,

 kestrels,

black caps and

reed warblers   189